The Itty Bitty Littles

Michelle Novak

Delilah,
Enjoy the magic!
Best Wishes,
Michelle

Printed by CreateSpace, An Amazon.com Company

Cover Design:

SelfPubBookCovers.com/9and3quarters

For Alyssa

Chapter One

Long ago, kings and queens slept in castles while villagers nested in cozy cottages within hamlets and farmers made small houses out of stones in their fields. Those were the places where people lived, but as for the forests and the vast lands of tall grasses that surrounded them, they remained wild.

Of course, most people knew about dragons and fairies, hobgoblins and elves, but there were other magical creatures too. There was one in particular that was almost never seen, and people hardly believed that it existed at all nor even knew *why* it should be called enchanted. For those people who claimed to have seen one, well, they had many ways of describing these beings, which were tiny indeed.

"I say, they look like brown seed puffs with scrawny bird legs." Said the farmer.

"They are *all* fur, a ball of it, and soft like a

rabbit!" Tooted the woodsman.

The falconer claimed, "Like little owlets they are, but not a beak to be seen!"

"They have eyes large and gleaming, like gold coins." Added the blacksmith.

And the baker had his say, "Soft and plump like a ball of risen dough."

But as for one sweet old woman, she called them itty-bitty-littles; itties, bitties or littles for short.

Lady Nettles lived in a cottage in vast wild grasses alongside of what was said to be an enchanted forest. Her little house was very old, made of timber and covered with a thatched roof woven from hay. The windows shut up with creaky wooden shutters and grey smoke, bringing with it the smells of good food, always rose from her chimney made of stacked stones. She'd grown up in the cottage with her parents, but now that she was old, she lived there all alone.

The closest village was not so very far away by horse, but it took well over an hour to get there on foot. There was a little dirt road, upon which people riding on horseback or travelers in their horse-drawn carriages rode. It passed through the field, just a short distance from Netty Nettles's cottage. She occasionally heard the trotting and neighing of passing horses, and remembered that there was a greater world outside of her cozy lodgings.

The nearby village was called Whistling Woods because it was built amidst beautiful trees, beneath which the townspeople enjoyed sitting and strolling whenever they had the time. Villagers would sometimes say that they could hear whistling in the trees when the wind blew, shaking the leaves upon their branches.

Now sometimes a farmer and his family lived far out in a quiet field where they could grow vegetables in their gardens and have plenty of room to keep their animals. And sometimes, a woodsman could be found dwelling at the edge of a thick forest within his own cabin made of ancient tree trunks. However, it was rare indeed that a kindly old woman should live all alone, on a plot carved out of the wilderness, without even a single neighbor to look in upon her. And so, the prattling wives of Whistling Woods sweetly chided Lady Nettles for living so far from town, making the long walk to her home in pairs, whenever they could manage a day away; couldn't she sell her cottage to a woodsman and find a little house in the village? Netty only laughed warmly and pushed the notion away with a flourish of her worn and helpful hands.

Chapter Two

The ladies in the village of Whistling Woods always did kind things for one another, and they also liked to meet together, sharing news with the energy of twittering spring birds! Therefore, it was a treat to break away from their chores in the village to bring a basket of good things to Lady Nettles, offering her some company while getting the chance to listen to some of her fascinating tales. The baskets they brought were not charity however, but rather items to trade with Netty, who was known to be an excellent craftswoman and cook!

For a warm knitted scarf or a kitten for a mouser, Lady Nettles traded with the ladies. She offered them crispy, buttery cookies filled with crunchy seeds and nuts, oaty muffins dotted with juicy berries, and fresh loaves of bread too. Netty also made fine smelling soaps which the village ladies couldn't get enough of, smelling of lavender, mint and rose. But what the women of Whistling Woods really loved were the old woman's teas, made from fresh herbs and flowers, which Netty grew and collected herself. She traded little sachets of her teas for the pleasant items that the village women brought her.

The women liked nothing more than to sit a spell in wooden chairs just outside of Netty's cottage door, amongst flowers afore the vast field of grasses, listening to the buzzing of insects, drinking tea and nibbling on Netty's cookies. It was there, or just before the old woman's hearth on colder days that they listened to her stories. Lady Nettles's visitors were entranced with every one of her words, for the woman was a very good storyteller.

There was the tale of the brownie that had once lived in Netty's cottage when she was just a little girl. Brownies were one sort of goblin, which most people described as little old men, quite ugly indeed, with wrinkles and bulbous noses! They dwelled with humans in their houses, but never more than one brownie in a home at a time. Though brownies liked to gather and gossip (much like the ladies of Whistling Woods), they preferred not to live too close to one another. Brownies often wore tiny vests and trousers made of leather, over cotton shirts. They liked their warm woolen hats and knitted socks too! They were said to stand hardly one foot tall, which made it easy for them to hide away in small places where no one ever looked. You see, they hid beneath loose floorboards, or within seldom used and cavernous butter crocks, even sometimes behind tall woodpiles near one's fireplace; anywhere they could comfortably sleep during the day and go unnoticed.

Brownies were kind goblins, which though not very handsome to look at, were good to families. They didn't pop out and frighten small children or grab women's toes in the night or tug at men's beards in their sleep. Those tricks were the sort of thing that other more troublesome kinds of goblins might like to play. These creatures had quite another purpose.

Brownies remained hidden all the day long, until after the sun went down and families were snoring in their beds. It was then that they came out and tidied what had gone undone in the day. They might wash a few bowls, sweep the crumbs from off the floor, or wipe down a table messy from supper. Or perhaps they would dust the mantle, darn a hole in a sock or peel a bucket of potatoes that were meant for next day's dinner. And for all of this, the lady of the house would leave the brownie good things to eat before she went off to bed each night, such as a slice of pie, a cup of fresh milk or hunks of bread and cheese. A smart woman always repaid the kindness of her household brownie.

However, there were some people who wouldn't spare even a morsel for their goblin to eat. If this were the case, brownies that were never known to play tricks, might turn naughty! Hungry and upset, they went tipping over sticky jars of fruity jam or spilled precious pots of honey, and then would run away to live in someone else's house.

Netty often told the tale of the brownie that had lived in her cottage, which she'd always suspected lived behind a loose board in the wall of the pantry. The small goblin helped her mother keep their home tidy and was especially good at polishing spoons and neatly stacking kindling for the fire. However, Netty's father was suspicious of *all* goblins, and didn't think it was right to live so close to *any* enchanted being. Goblins, like other elflike creatures, were said to be magical. Some people said that rather than doing their chores with their hands, with one magical wink the work was done, allowing them plenty of time to get warm by the fire and enjoy the meals left out for them. Netty had never actually seen their brownie, let alone watched him polish a spoon, so she had no idea how they got the work done.

Lady Nettles's father told his good wife to send the brownie off, in the kindest way. And so, Netty's mother sewed a brand-new set of clothing, an outfit made of smooth leather and soft cotton, to fit a being about one foot tall. Her mother hadn't seen the goblin either, so could only do her best, not quite knowing his exact size. Inside of a tiny pocket in a vest she made for him, she placed a miniature white handkerchief, for when he may have to sneeze. And inside a rough fabric sack tied to a twig, she placed a square of honeycomb, a handful of plump raspberries and walnuts, and a *tiny* loaf of bread. Netty watched her mother forlornly that night as she placed out the gifts before bedtime.

The very next morning, no small chore was noticed to have been done. The brownie was gone forever. Netty's father was satisfied. Though it left more cleaning to his wife, he felt it was best that only *people* lived in their house. At the very least, they'd sent the brownie off the proper way; making him something new to wear cued him to take a journey and find a new home. Netty hoped he'd find a generous one and soon; though she'd never met him, he'd seemed like such a helpful goblin.

Chapter Three

There was another beloved story, one that gave Lady Nettles's visitors a merry laugh every time they heard it! One lovely summer's day, a cloud of fairies made one terrible mess in Netty's cottage. It was a sunny afternoon and the breeze was soft and warm, the grasses swayed in the wind and the leaves rustled on their branches at the forest's edge. With it being such a delightful day, Netty craved some sun on her face and to soak a little warmth into her aged bones. She would spend some time in the field, taking with her a basket and a pair of shears so that she could collect useful herbs, edible mushrooms and fragrant flowers. Perhaps she would find some special plants for her teas and soaps. Lady Nettles felt certain that it would be safe to leave her shutters open wide that day, as curious raccoons only came out at night and Netty had yet to ever meet a human thief. With her windows open wide, a

12

fine breeze would circulate through her home, bringing a bit of summer indoors.

Netty knew that fairies were as real as sparrows and spiders, for she had seen one more than once! However, they were so small and swift as they flitted about, that she rarely got a good look. On the occasion that she'd spied one, as fast and wee as a hummingbird, she admired their wings, as iridescent and colorful as a dragonfly's. She'd glimpse one, hovering with curiosity over a perfumed blossom in her garden. Sometimes it landed just long enough for her to admire. How magical were their delicate elfish ears, their clothes decorated with soft petals and downy bird feathers, and their pretty faces, whether boy fairy or girl! They had bits of green moss and the smallest buds that could be found in the field, weaved into their messy tresses. Lady Nettles didn't believe that fairies *ever* brushed their hair. Their locks were playful and messy, filled with braids and tiny found objects from the forest. This should not have been wholly surprising however, as there was a phenomenon well-known to all; fairy locks.

When people, especially children, fell asleep at night with combed hair and then woke the next morning with wild knots, loose braids and difficult to brush tangles, it was said that fairies had snuck into the home while everyone slept. Faes had always loved dancing on people's heads, causing them to have lively and colorful dreams, and one unmanageable head of hair the next morning! Whether the fairies thought it was a merry trick, or that they genuinely thought people would enjoy their new hairstyles, no one knew.

On that summer's day, Netty left home with her basket and had one pleasant afternoon out-of-doors. At dusk however, her delight turned to dismay when returning to her cottage to stoke her evening fire and make her supper, she stumbled upon quite a sight!

Scattered upon her table were blue juniper berries, many smashed. She lit a candle and eyeing the messy fruit up-close, discovered teensy footprints. But this was not all. There were soft white feathers dropped in places on the floor, and a jug filled with the juice of apples spilled, a fruity smelling pool on the ground. She found the jug's cork rolled far away under a chair. A basket filled with colorful lambswool yarn was disturbed, several spools uncoiled upon her bed. Her rounds of pink and blue yarn were missing entirely. She couldn't find her sewing needles or her silver thimble; her polished looking glass was also nowhere to be found. A gooseberry pie, left uncovered in her pantry, was trampled upon. Crumbs and fruity sauce, sticky and sweet, were smeared all over the shelf; the pie was ruined. And just outside of her front door, one of Netty's egg-laying hens was making quite a fuss. Walking out to see what all of the ruckus was about, she found the chicken's belly half plucked of its airy down feathers. The hen would grow them back eventually, but for now she seemed terribly nervous over what had happened to her. She'd usually be following Netty around, clucking for some breadcrumbs, but instead was keeping her distance and jumping at the sound of every passing cricket.

Lady Nettles shook her head with disappointment; what a mess she'd found, and what a waste of a good pie! About to head back inside to start cleaning up her cottage, she heard a hissing and a growling coming from her toolshed, which stood next to her garden. The door of the small outbuilding was open wide. It was beginning to grow dark outside, so she went for a glass lantern and lit a sturdy wax candle within it.

As she entered into her shed, she found

her cat Sunshine having a fit. Netty had named her cat thus because she was all fluffy and white with one large round of orange on her coat, which looked like the sun. Sunshine was not alone. Lady Nettles's cat had cornered a boy fairy that now stood fluttering its wings, hopeful to get away. The cat batted its claws before the creature, hissing all the while, keeping her catch pinned to the wall. It seemed cats hunted far more than birds and mice!

As careful as could be, Netty scooped up Sunshine into one arm while still holding up the lantern with the other. The fairy stood for a moment longer as it tried to catch its breath, a faint and glittering glow silhouetted around its tiny frame. And then, in an instant, the fairy lifted off from the ground and flew towards the door. Sunshine swatted into the open air with a guttural growl as it did, but the fairy got away. The cat swayed its tail in agitation for having missed out on capturing its prey, but was soon purring in Netty's loving arms as they walked toward the cottage for a little supper.

Over the next few weeks, Netty made some unique discoveries in the field and forest around her home. There were soft nests of white hen feathers interwoven with pliable twigs atop saplings, blue and pink yarn strung between tree branches, teeny handprints on a rock the color of juniper berries (several discarded berries squished and scattered near the stone). She even found one of her shiny spoons hanging from a string of blue yarn in a sturdy bush; a utensil she hadn't even noticed was missing. Netty could tell that a great many fairies had invaded her home that summer's day, the last of which had been very lucky to escape!

When people heard this tale, listeners often wondered if Netty hadn't been tempted to catch the cornered boy fairy. After all, how many people in the village of Whistling Woods alone would have paid a coin to see a live fairy; surely many! To see a fairy was rare, they were just too cunning and quick! Besides, after collecting a basketful of money, she could have let the fairy go. No doubt he'd warn the rest of the fairies to steer clear of human homes, they'd dare not make mischief again.

Lady Nettles only waved away these little plots with a chuckle. First of all, fairies were so clever; it would have escaped before she'd collected a single gold piece, no matter how she'd caged it. Miffed over its capture, it would have brought a cloud of fairies back to cause more trouble around her cottage. But more importantly, Netty didn't believe that *any* creature should endure imprisonment. Even her hens, her goat named Sally, and Sunshine roamed free as they liked. This was perhaps why even she herself had never moved into the village, remaining near the wild; it was there that Lady Nettles felt most free.

Chapter Four

Netty shared her stories of benevolent brownies and rascally faes with her village visitors and entertained travelers stopping at her door for a pinch of hospitality with other tales too. There was the mermaid-like water sprite that she'd unexpectedly found singing in a stream just a short distance into the forest, and that horrible roar she'd heard coming from a deep cave even further into the woods, which she was certain came from a small species of rock dragon still rumored to live in the area. But of all the stories of enchanted creatures that she'd stored up over the years, there was one tale that people asked to hear most. Wouldn't she tell them about the itty-bitty-littles?

On a spring day several years before, when Netty was a little more spry and her joints ached less, she spent a chilly but bright morning preparing her garden for planting.

Netty lived on the fruit and vegetables of her garden and tended to her plot of earth with great care. With her fresh produce, her hens' eggs, the milk from Sally the goat and honey from a hive of bees she kept, Lady Nettles ate quite well. These with the seeds, nuts, edible flowers and sweet berries collected from the wilderness around her, she was able to bake the best breads and biscuits, to churn the freshest butter and to make the most delicious fruit spreads. Netty even knew how to hunt for all kinds of mushrooms, to make the most amazing soups and egg dishes anyone could ever hope to eat.

As she worked a small shovel into the dirt of her square garden, turning over the hard earth that spring day, her chickens came running to scratch up the earthworms and beetles. They ran around energetically, just as hens do, having quick conversations with one another by clucking and squawking loudly.

When her work was done and the plot ready to accept seeds, Netty looked to the sky just as a cold wind came over her and her chickens (whose feathers blew this way and that on their bodies). There were clouds approaching, grey and ominous. Lady Nettles knew right then that today was not the day to drop her seeds into the earth. The storm that was coming might bring snow, and perhaps even freeze the ground once more, destroying her seeds so that they would not grow. True spring had not come as early as she'd thought.

The wind grew stronger and the sun quickly faded away behind the billowy clouds, the last of the day's warmth disappearing with it. The chickens began clucking far more loudly, their feathers ruffled as they ran in circles; they could also tell that a storm was coming, and fast!

Netty knew that it was time to usher her hens into their shelter and make her way inside herself; there was no time to lose. She would place several large logs upon her fire and make a blaze; wouldn't a hot pot of tea and some crispy toast sound good! Cozy in her cabin, she would wait out the storm very pleasantly. Soon safely in their henhouse, Netty hurried into her house, shivering with a chill and wiping her windblown hair out of her eyes. Just as she approached her fireplace, she remembered the goat! Her beloved Sally was still roaming free. Of course, so was Sunshine the cat, but that clever creature had never failed to find a warm and secure place to hide.

Every morning, Netty opened the gate surrounding Sally's roofed and roomy goat house, filled with plenty of dry hay to sleep upon, and where the goat was safe at night when more dangerous animals lurked about. Once the sun went down each evening, she couldn't chance that a wolf might try to gobble up Sally, and so secured her in her pen. But now, as it was only midday, who knew where Sally was off exploring? Perhaps she was nibbling grass in the field, or green leaves from bushes around the woods. She might even be foraging within the forest, chomping on sappy tree bark, which was one of her favorite foods.

Netty opened her shutters and peeked outside. Everything was blowing; even one of her dishrags hanging limply on her clothesline plucked off and flew away. Tiny snowflakes, though still sparse, foretold the blizzard that was approaching. There was no Sally to be seen; oh what should she do? Netty knew of course that her precious goat could not be left alone out in a storm. Sally could get lost and even freeze. Netty imagined her goat lonesome in a snowdrift, bleating to the wind. Oh no!

Hurrying, Lady Nettles threw the warmest wool shawl that she owned over her head and shoulders, wrapping it tightly around her. She also pulled thick knitted gloves over her hands and then ran out of the door. The wind was blowing more strongly than before and the snow began falling more heavily with each second; large flakes melted on Netty's face and blew into her eyes. Winter storms could stir up so quickly, and become dangerous very fast. Soon, all would be white and it would be hard to see. If far out in the field, it was even possible to become lost, hardly able to tell the difference between the white ground and sky. What a horrible thing if Netty were to lose her way in the snow! But she still had time; she just needed to find that goat!

First, she searched all around her yard and then scurried out into the vast open field of grass. She strained to listen for the call of her goat, but couldn't hear any bleating. Swift as she could, she swept along the edge of the field and called out to her goat, stopping to listen for any response. There was nothing. The snow continued to fall harder and harder. Was Sally in the enchanted forest? The storm was blustery and Netty was getting colder by the minute. She would have to enter the woods in search of her goat.

Entering the forest, the ground was thick with brush, roots and rocks. The walk was made more slippery because of the snow, and Netty stumbled some as she made her way. Looking around frantically, she called out to Sally. Walking more deeply into the woods, she wondered if she'd have to give up the search before long. The sky was growing darker, the snow was falling heavily and it was cold. But how could she leave her pet behind? She called and called until she'd nearly given up hope. It was then that she finally heard something. There was a goat's reply, "Baahh…beehhhhhh." The sound was faint, but Netty went in its direction.

Pausing for a moment to listen once more, she thought that it sounded like the bleating of the goat was echoing. How could that be? Was it an effect of the storm? Or perhaps her goat was calling from within one of the many rock caves in the forest? She yelled out to Sally and heard the reply again. She could distinctly hear Sally's bleating, and then what sounded like a dozen or so smaller bleats, as though there was an entire pen of baby goats! It was certainly the storm playing tricks on her ears. There was one thing she knew however, she'd soon find her goat and they could head home to safety.

Finally, she spied her beloved friend, standing aside a mound of snow-covered rocks, slightly protected by an overgrowth of thick bushes. Netty was so relieved that she called out to Sally with happiness. The goat bleated forcefully in return, a fear melting from its eyes now that she'd seen Netty too. Only, Sally's call was immediately followed by a handful of odd-sounding, stressed and tiny bleats! What *was* that?

Chapter Five

Netty drew nearer and found that Sally looked strange. The orange-brown fur at her belly had always been short. But just now, it appeared to be so long that it skirted the ground! Surely a goat's fur grew no faster than any other creature's. As Netty scrunched her eyes, focusing in on a better look of her goat, it seemed to her that there was in fact a second animal taking shelter beneath Sally; the goat was protecting another creature from the snow and wind. It made the most sense that it should be a baby goat, why else would the animal bleat *like* a goat? This was puzzling however, as Sally certainly hadn't birthed one herself and all of Netty's neighbors who owned goats themselves, lived a great distance away; too far for a baby goat to walk.

Now standing just before Sally, Netty blinked with disbelief at the mass of fur huddled beneath her goat. She couldn't make it out; it was just one large ball of fuzz! What on earth could it be? A golden fox? A light brown lamb? An enormous orange cat fat on field mice? This was absurd!

"Hey you there!" Lady Nettles honked, hoping to stir the creature taking refuge beneath her goat. Sally was excited to hear Netty's voice; she wagged her short stubby tail and *baahhed*. All at once, another sprinkling of tiny bleats began, and it was coming from the ball of fuzz. It seemed to be mimicking the very sound that the goat was making. And then, there were eyes! One set and then two, then eight and then twelve sets of large eyes! Netty blinked with surprise, and the eyes did too.

It was then that something even more surprising happened. An orb of fur detached itself from the whole, with its two big eyes in the middle of its body and a pair of birdlike little legs and feet appearing. It was about the size of a large apple. It began walking around the snow before Sally, leaving tiny tracks. Another ball of fur did the same, and then another, until there were many creatures walking in a dazed circle. Netty could see that some were shivering from the cold. A few stood completely still, drawing up one foot or other into their bodies for warmth.

Netty had fallen upon a brood of *itty-bitty-littles*! She'd heard tales of them before, called by many names, but was hardly sure whether she herself had ever seen one. Sometimes she suspected that she'd spied an itty peeking out at her from a tree nook or thicket of brush, but littles were so elusive, and even magical some said. Most people never saw one, especially if they lived in a crowded village. Netty hadn't been sure if it had been other animals she'd seen watching her from the woods altogether.

The littles were clearly confused. Netty had heard that bitties hibernated in the winter, as many animals do, only coming out in spring and hiding away in autumn once more. Had the itties come out of hibernation too soon, becoming overwhelmed by this unexpected winter storm? It was very possible, even Netty had thought that spring was officially started and that winter was gone for good.

Sally bleated again, walking towards Lady Nettles. The littles bleated too and all at once, began following after the goat. One slipped on the snow and fell down, rolling for a moment and then kicking awkwardly as it bleated loudly. It was instantly clear to Netty that the bitties could not last for long in this weather, as tiny and fragile as they were, like kittens. There was only one thing to do. Removing her shawl, she began gathering the precious itties one by one, placing them into her warm garment as delicately as possible. One in hand, she looked at it up-close and it blinked with its enormous eyes, eyes just like an owl's. It spread wide its tiny clawed toes, helpless in Netty's hand. Soon she had a squirming, fuzzy bundle in her arms. A dozen little bleats sounded out each time Sally made a peep. Netty thought that it was curious that itty-bitty-littles bleated, though she didn't know what sort of sound she'd expected that they made. No mouths could be seen at first glance, they looked like creatures that would make no noise at all.

With her goat beside her, they soon made their way back to the cottage through the wind and snow. Netty led Sally to her goat house and gave her a bowl of dry oats, still clinging to her bundle. She then closed up the pen and took the itties inside with her. Taking up a big basket, she gently placed the bundle, woolen shawl and all within it. The knitted cover fell away over the sides of the basket and once more, Lady Nettles was met with twelve sets of enormous golden eyes and adorable fuzzy bodies.

Perhaps they were hungry, but what did they eat? The cabin was cold, so Netty set out to build up the fire. She wasn't sure how to care for her new wards, now snuggling together in their man-made refuge. One by one, the little pairs of eyes closed and the littles drew up their feet, nesting into themselves. Their exertions out in the storm had exhausted them. And so, there in their basket upon Netty's shawl, the itties fell asleep before the fire.

Chapter Six

Lady Nettles slowly opened her eyes to a new day, having slept soundly after all that had happened the day before. As she did, she was met with quite a surprise! Twelve balls of fur stood staring at her as she lay unmoving, silent and blinking their large eyes as they watched her. Though slightly startled to find so many little creatures standing around (and even upon) her, she couldn't help but laugh and began chuckling aloud. In response, the itty-bitty-littles repeated the sound of her laughter; tiny voices began replicating her chuckles awkwardly. It didn't sound exactly how Netty's laughter did, but their talent impressed her! It seemed that they could repeat the sounds that they heard around them, first Sally's bleating and now Netty's chuckling. She'd first assumed that littles made a similar sound to goats, but now understood that they could make a great many more noises than that. Lady Nettles laughed again more boisterously, shaking the bed. The littles did too and a few jumped up and down on their little chicken legs, one walking round in a circle. Some blinked fast and others slow, a few hopped off of the bed and began running around the cottage.

Netty smiled at the adorable creatures as she sat up in bed, trying not to throw an itty off balance as she peeled away the bedcovers. The remaining littles began jumping off the bed and then scattered.

Just then, a songbird whistled from without one of the windows. Wrapping a fresh shawl over the shoulders of her nightgown, Netty walked over to the window and opened the shutters. It was a bright, sunny day and the storm had passed. There was a thick layer of snow on the ground. It was time for Netty's morning chores. There was the fire to stoke, breakfast to make, dishes to do, and sweeping too! Then she had the chickens to water and feed, and Sally to let loose to roam the yard once more for her nibbles. Today she'd have to give her goat some extra breakfast scraps since the snow was so thick; Sally would have trouble foraging for enough to fill her.

Shutting the shutters again to keep out the cold, she walked toward her dressing cabinet for a change of clothes. As she passed the basket where the itties had slept before the fire, she noticed something moving upon the shawl that was still inside. With all the itty-bitty-littles exploring the room, the basket should have been empty. Were her eyes playing tricks on her? It didn't seem like the movement of a single creature, but many! Moving toward the basket, she wondered if she didn't have mice in her house; they liked getting out of the cold and into warm houses too. A basketful however, would be strange indeed. Netty stood over the basket and peered inside, she could *not* believe her eyes. Baby itty-bitty-littles no larger than coins!

"Oh heavens!" Lady Nettles cried out. The newborns became startled and ran altogether to one side of the basket. They huddled together as one ball of fur, much the same way as she'd found the larger itties taking shelter beneath her goat. Meanwhile, a cacophony of noise rang out from the other creatures around the room, like little voices attempting to replicate the words 'oh' and 'heavens'. The words were not distinct, but Netty knew that they were mimicking her.

Several littles quickly ran over to the basket and peeked inside. One hopped over the side and hurried toward the babies, who broke from their huddle and squeezed against the larger itty. Perhaps this was their mother. Teeny-tiny *cheep-cheep* sounds could then be heard; they sounded like baby birds. What a sight!

Had it been a warmer day, Netty would have opened the door and let the itties run free. After all, they were wild creatures that belonged out-of-doors, not in a house. But as cold as it was, and with all of that snow, where would the littles go, and with a flock of itty-*itty*-bitty-littles too? These creatures certainly had come out of their place of hibernation far too soon. Netty could only hope that spring would melt all the snow and show its lovely face once more, and quickly too!

Chapter Seven

With a house full of itties, Netty's cottage was exciting and a little bit noisy. However, she took joy in hosting such a special bunch and went about her daily chores. As she washed her dishes, two itties found their way up upon the side of her washing bucket to watch her wash, blinking all the while. Drying a plate with her apron, she went to put the clean dish away in the cupboard. When she turned around again, one of the two itties was walking inside of her rinsing bucket, which was only about an inch deep in water. The other little, still standing on the rim of the wash bucket made an adorable chirping noise like a sparrow and then hopped over and into the rinsing bucket to join his friend.

They began playing by making little splashes with their feet. The water quickly started to sop their light brown fur, until Netty was amused to see two very wet, birdlike creatures before her. Tiny beaks and winglike appendages bare of any feathers; parts of their bodies normally disguised. Lady Nettles had wondered how they created sound, and even how they ate for that matter, but hadn't seen beneath their fur to know whether they had beaks, mouths or snouts! She thought they must be creatures of the bird realm; they looked like skinny wet chickens to her. However, birds laid eggs and not live young. How did one produce a basket full of babies if it was a bird? Also, they had fur and not feathers. How perplexing itty-bitty-littles were!

Soon jumping back up onto the bucket's rim, both itties shook the water from their bodies the way that dogs do. Within a few minutes more, while Netty finished her dishes, the bitties were dry and as fluffy as ever.

Soon sitting to her breakfast of wild herb tea, eggs and biscuits with butter, the itties all began to hurry toward her table. She still didn't know what bitties ate, but assumed it was much the same things that a chicken might peck at, such as bugs, plants and seeds. Many of the littles stood watching Netty from their places on the floor as she buttered her first biscuit, their wide eyes blinking. But then, several jumped up upon an empty chair aside her, and next onto the tabletop. They were followed by more itties. In a flash, they were ravenously pecking at her biscuits like a flock of pigeons fighting over a fistful of grain. As they did, they trampled her butter and began picking and scratching at part of a loaf of bread sitting on a plate on the table. They gobbled up everything before them, one even hovering over a wooden cup of her water, dipping its hidden beak into it and then putting its head back to swallow. It repeated this several times.

Netty had been so surprised, that she'd simply watched the bitties feast, not quite sure what to do. She didn't want to frighten the creatures by shooing them away, but they had become wild over her breakfast and were leaving none for her! Just then, an itty knocked over her teacup. Warm tea spilled into a puddle on the table and more than one itty walked right through it, leaving clawed tracks of tea on her tablecloth as they went. The cup rolled off the table, landing in a shatter on the floor.

"Oh, no!" Netty cried loudly. She didn't have very many teacups, what a shame! Pausing when they heard her holler, the littles all looked at Netty in unison.

"Oh, no, no, oh! No, no, oh, oh." Came the repetitious responses. Things were getting crazy! The itties continued to peep wildly as they ran around the table. Netty bent over to pick up a few pieces of her precious cup, laying the shards before her on the table.

"Oh, no." She said once more, this time with a sigh and a click of her tongue. She wished she hadn't lost such a nice cup. Some of the littles made clicking noises too, which grated on Netty's nerves. Others stopped running and stood silently observing her as she scooted a few of the pieces of the cup together, but it was hopeless to mend. After a minute of sitting silently, she got up the energy to clean this newly made mess; the itties had all grown quiet and once again stood watching her. It was then that one of the littles did something very curious.

Approaching the large shards that Netty had just puzzled together, an itty hovered over the pieces. First closing its eyes, it then sat down upon the pieces of her broken teacup. Did it think the rounded white porcelain pieces were eggs to nest upon and keep warm? The others silently watched as the itty began purring like a cat, the creature's fur vibrated with the tremulous sound. At that moment, something unbelievable and certainly magical occurred. The itty rose up, but not on its feet. It was sitting on a *new* cup, the old shards pushed away. A new teacup had produced out of thin air!

Was it *possible* for an animal to make a teacup? This was far stranger than anything Netty had ever seen, and she worried that the itties had enchanted her, making her see things that weren't real. But then, two more littles on the floor and another upon the table also squatted over broken pieces of her cup, the purring substantially louder. In the blink of an eye, Lady Nettles had four new teacups! Each looked everything like the original, with even a tiny crack on each lip as the first had had. Four cups, produced from a single cup, brought about by the magic of itties. How could this be? But Netty hadn't another moment to ponder over what she'd seen, as a frantic knocking came to her door. Standing, she wiped tea and crumbs from her apron and headed towards the door.

Chapter Eight

Lady Nettles opened the cottage door just a few inches so that she could peek out to get a look at who was knocking.

"Who is there?" She called out.

A lady's voice answered her. "I am a noblewoman's maid, my lady."

Netty could see that it was a young woman at the door, perhaps just 16 or 17 years old. She opened the door just a little further to get a better view.

"I see, and from where did you come, young lady?" Netty asked.

The girl smiled warmly, looking relieved to see Lady Nettles.

"Ah, good day madam. My name is Heidiwink, a lady's maid to Countess Bramblenook of Bloomshire."

The girl's head was covered in a hooded green cape and the face that looked out from it was very pretty, her cheeks rosy from the cold.

Netty wondered over the girl's name. She'd heard the name Heidi before, but Heidiwink was new to her. Neither had she ever heard of the town of Bloomshire. But this was no matter, a foreign name from a faraway place; the world was vast and Netty had only gone so far as Whistling Woods.

"Pray tell, how did you find my door and what business do you have with me?" The old woman inquired.

The girl's lovely smile turned into a forlorn look. The change was almost too dramatic.

"The carriage that we were riding in was overtaken by yesterday's storm. We are traveling, you see. We were on the road nearby, not far from your cottage when the snow began swirling so thickly and the wind blowing so fiercely, that we were unable to drive on. The Countess, coachman and I spent one very frightening night within the carriage. The horses stood outside, covered only by several wool blankets, which the coachman had had thrown over his own lap during our journey. It was too dangerous to stray from the carriage on foot in search of another shelter, though if we'd known how close your house was, we might have tried. It was truly a blizzard, my lady."

Netty nodded in agreement, the weather had certainly been fierce.

Heidiwink smiled once more as she continued, "But now the sun is shining and our driver is digging out the carriage so that we can continue on our way. Only, my mistress, Countess Bramblenook sent me out to see if there weren't any cottages close by, from which we could buy a bite to eat. We are all very hungry after such a cold and perilous night. The horses the most, I'm sure. Can you not spare any victuals for us famished travelers madam? I have money, of course."

Netty thought she saw something curious

just then, beneath the girl's velvet green hood. One of her ears was visible amidst her head of curly dark locks, and the very tip of it at the top, looked *pointy*. Heidiwink seemed to notice that Netty was eyeing her closely and quickly moved her hand, pushing a tuft of hair over her ear. The old woman thought that this was very odd, but perhaps it had just been the shadows beneath the girl's hood playing tricks on her eyes.

"Well now, you poor dears! I imagine that it was a very trying night for you all. How exhausted you must be." Lady Nettles chirped with sympathy. But as she observed the girl's face, it didn't seem to her to look all that worn and tired. Heidiwink certainly didn't look as disheveled as one would expect, after a long journey and a sleepless night in a horse-drawn carriage. In fact, the girl looked quite rested, her face and hair seemed flawless.

Though Netty couldn't shake the feeling

that something seemed out of place, she said, "I'll just go take a look in my pantry and see what there is to spare. I would invite you in to stand a moment by my fire, but I have a...visitor. A sick friend, whom I would rather not have disturbed, as she is sleeping just now."

She felt instantly guilty over having told a lie, even to a stranger. Lady Nettles believed in honesty and never had a reason to tell a fib to anyone. However, with all those itty-bitty-littles running around the cottage making a mess (she thought she'd just heard something else crashing to the floor), it wasn't the best idea to invite anyone in just now.

"Of course," said the girl with a smile and a nod, "I'll just wait right here."

Chapter Nine

Netty retreated into her house, closing the door behind her. The itties were everywhere! Snoozing in her bed, finishing off the last of her breakfast crumbs upon the table, even splashing and jumping in and out of her washing buckets, mimicking all sorts of sounds that they'd picked up in the forest. It was clear that littles were no more meant to live in cottages than squirrels were. If the bitties hadn't had a brood of babies, and if it were not so very cold and snowy outside, she'd have been tempted to shoo them from her house this instant, back outside where they belonged.

Lady Nettles quickly plucked a few items that she could spare from her pantry: the last of yesterday's early morning baking, a few knobby carrots, and a handful of hard-boiled eggs. She bound everything up in a cotton cloth and hurried back towards the door. Unexpectedly, she found Heidiwink standing inside with the door shut.

The girl looked around at all the chaos unfolding around them and smiled. Netty would have expected anyone that had come upon this scene to look shocked, or even to shriek! Though people told tales about the existence of itty-bitty-littles, to actually see one would be surprising. Here, Netty had an entire house astir with the creatures, and they weren't being elusive at all!

The girl's smile faded and she quickly feigned astonishment, drawing her hand up over her mouth with a gasp. "Why madam! Are these wild things what I think they are?"

"Why mistress, you shouldn't have come into the house uninvited." Netty sighed, exasperated with all of the commotion. What a morning! "It wasn't polite to enter my home without being asked." She scolded, clutching the bundle of food to her apron.

"I heard a ruckus coming from inside and

thought that you may be in trouble!" Heidiwink explained. "When you didn't invite me in, I waited patiently but then heard such strange noises. I thought I would just peek inside and see if all was well. I *hope* you aren't upset. If there *had* been a bandit making trouble for you, I might have saved your life!"

Lady Nettles still couldn't believe the girl's boldness, nor did she believe that Heidiwink was being sincere with her excuse. She couldn't shake the feeling that the girl was up to something.

The lady's maid looked merrily around the room until her eyes caught hold of the basket and she squealed with delight. "Bantling bitties too?" Madame, where did you come about these littles?"

Netty shrugged, too overwhelmed but to tell the truth and hope that the girl would soon be on her way. "If you must know, they were caught up in the storm, much as you were. I sheltered them last night, but as soon as the snow melts and the temperature rises, back to their wilderness they'll go!"

Heidiwink giggled at the flurry of fuzzy activity. "Hmmm, but don't you know an itty-bitty's worth my lady? Haven't you heard? They are magical! Hasn't a single little done anything out of the ordinary since you rescued them?"

Lady Nettles didn't like this at all. Of course people said that these creatures had magic abilities, but unless you'd seen it for yourself, it was just nonsense. Netty would never have believed it herself if it hadn't been for the teacups. What was Heidiwink getting at?

"And what kind of magic would that be, young lady?" Netty questioned. She was growing nervous for her houseguests and wanted Heidiwink to leave.

"I've heard that they can triple men's gold,

sitting upon treasure to multiply it!" The girl blurted, looking greedily upon the basket full of tiny itties near the hearth.

Netty forced a chuckle, "Ha-ha! What silly stories fools tell! Can't you see that they are only creatures of the forest? Like any rabbit or bird? They may be rare to see, but magic they aren't!"

Once more, she hated the lie and blushed. She felt however, that the girl was out of place and that the itties might be in danger. After all, a magical creature was a very powerful thing. If a person harnessed magic, a gift they were not given to begin with, who knew what terrible, greedy things they might do with it? Further, Netty did not believe in trapping any creature in order to abuse it for its natural abilities. No matter how magical, no fairy, nor itty, deserved to be in the hands of people.

"Perhaps you are right, and itties hold no power. Nevertheless, I'll give you 10 gold coins for my choice of just one of those offspring. I adore kittens and puppies; won't one of those make such a darling pet?" Heidiwink held an endearing smile upon her face.

Drawing upon what she knew to be right, the old woman refused outright, however kindly. "10 gold pieces is a fortune for a lady's maid. I assure you that your spending so much on such an ordinary creature of the forest is not worth ruining your savings for. Such a wild creature will grow irritating and tedious to you; can't you see how much energy they have?" Netty knew it to be a great sum, one that a young lady who was not a noble herself, could never offer.

Heidiwink replied sharply, "But that is for *me* to decide, no? You live so humbly here, what grand comforts you could afford with those 10 gold coins."

Lady Nettles thumped her foot and all the littles halted in their places, even Heidiwink looked surprised. "That may be so, but the answer is *no*. It is now time that you be on your way. Surely your carriage is now free from the snow, your mistress awaits. But as I would not see anyone hungry, I give you this food as a gift. I won't take anything for it."

Chapter Ten

What happened next proved more magical that anything Netty could have imagined. Owing to the greed and persistence that she'd felt coming from the young lady, she'd wanted her on her way. After all, she had witnessed how magical itty-bitty-littles were and wanted to protect them. With even a single one of these creatures, Heidiwink could have made a fortune, the enchanted animal suffering all the while, far away from its home. If these beings could multiply teacups, they could squat upon a gold piece and make a mound of gold. If they could replicate every noise around them, they could be made to repeat words like parrots for amusement. It would be unbearable to see even one of these creatures, however rambunctious and troublesome they might be, in any person's hands.

Lowering the plush cloth of her emerald hood, the girl's eyes sparkled unnaturally.

Tucking her curls behind her ears, Netty could clearly see that they were indeed pointy. The lady was so fair, her skin increasingly luminous by the second, that the old woman's mouth gaped open. Heidiwink began speaking in a melodious language that Netty had never heard before, and scanning around the room, as if directing her words to the littles. The itties began singing, chirping and tooting. It was joyful to the ears, a language only they understood. With a flourish of one of her hands, which faintly seemed to glow, the itty-bitty-littles began to herd toward the young lady. The hatchlings remained in their basket, too tiny to jump out, but could be heard peeping energetically.

Lady Nettles knew at once that this was no girl, but an elf. And if the lore was true, this elfish woman might not have been so young at all, but ancient indeed. Elves were beautiful, and they were magical, but they were tricky too. Netty might have given in to Heidiwink's charming pleas, trading an itty-bitty-little for gold. But her true heart had stood firm, no match even for an enchanting elf. She sat the cloth full of food down on a small table close by; it wouldn't be needed.

"Kind madam, Mistress Nettles...thank you for watching over *ours*. This shows that not every human is filled with greed; there is also much goodness amongst you. Surely you saw one of these creatures multiply something, whether it was an object of worth or not. You can see how precious our beloved littles are. That basket of infants there came about the same way. Without a birth, or an egg to sit upon, littles can instantly produce more of themselves out of pure love. That is their magic. They are too wild, too generous, and *too* beloved by elves to be a part of your world. But as you would not be tempted with gold, I think you understand."

Heidiwink opened the door and stood to one side of the threshold. As she did, a path of snow leading away from the cottage began to melt into the ground. Presumably the path would lead deep into the forest, to the secret place where enchanted creatures lived. The itties filed out one by one into the sunny new day onto the path. Netty saw a few tufts of green and purple pop out from the ground along the path, spring flowers. And then, from either side of her door, fairies flew into the cottage! The bewitching elf directed them with her beautiful language. It looked to Lady Nettles that there were at least twenty tiny beings, their incandescent wings fluttering in a flurry of colors. They flew directly to the basket filled with tiny peeping littles, picked it up and carried it away with them.

One fairy broke off from the rest and flew directly before Netty's face. She crossed her eyes to get a better look of the miniature being, who hovered just before her nose. She couldn't believe it! It was the boy fairy that she had saved from Sunshine's claws that summer's day! For a second, she was a little nervous. What was the fairy boy planning? She'd heard of people receiving a pinch to the tip of their nose, or a tug to an ear after surprising or grabbing for a fairy. Instead, the fairy boy hovered close to Netty's cheek. She could feel a soft flutter and beating wind at her face. The wee creature placed his tiny hands upon her soft cheek, and kissed it! He was thanking her for saving his life.

The fairy boy zipped out of the door toward the basket floating away above the magical spring path. With that, all fairies, and all itty-bitty-littles were gone. They were on their way home. All that was left was the elf woman, who with a slight curtsey to Lady Nettles, replaced her fine velvet hood back over her head and trailed down the fresh lane, away from the cottage. As she did, more flowers sprung up of every color, and ferns too unfurled their green leaves; the edges of the path became plush with plants. For a time, Netty stood at the door admiring the magical lane. And soon, she could no longer see the elf woman, who disappeared out of sight.

When Netty went back into her cottage, she was shocked to find that all was returned to normal, not even the smallest mess to be found. Further, the cottage was tidier than it had been before she'd brought the littles home with her. Eyeing her shelf of teacups, she found eight altogether, when only yesterday, she'd only owned three. She now had plenty of teacups to serve her guests with. The food she'd intended to give to Heidiwink was back in the pantry and a hot plate of breakfast was sitting out for her, a few fragrant blossoms decorated the table in a pretty glass vase that Netty had never seen before. And there beside it also, was a small green velvet bag. Sitting down to her morning meal, she opened the surprisingly heavy sack and looked inside. There were 10 gold coins, a gift to be put toward the comforts of a good old woman. How Heidiwink had done all of this, well that was magic of course. And what a magical story this was soon to make for all of the friends who came to visit Netty Nettles from the neighboring village of Whistling Woods!

The Itty Bitty Littles

24888126R00043

Made in the USA
Columbia, SC
30 August 2018